THE ROAD TO SINHARAT

THE ROAD TO SINHARAT

by Leigh Brackett

The people of Mars were perverse. They did not want Earth's proffer of rich land, much water, new power. They fought rehabilitation. And with them fought Carey, the Earthman who wanted only the secret that lay at the end of the road to Sinharat.

I

The door was low, deep-sunk into the thickness of the wall. Carey knocked and then he waited, stooped a bit under the lintel stone, fitting his body to the meager shadow as though he could really hide it there. A few yards away, beyond cracked and tilted paving-blocks, the Jekkara Low Canal showed its still black water to the still black sky, and both were full of stars.

Nothing moved along the canal site. The town was closed tight, and this in itself was so unnatural that it made Carey shiver. He had been here before and he knew how it ought to be. The chief industry of the Low Canal towns is sinning of one sort or another, and they work at it right around the clock. One might have thought that all the people had gone away, but Carey knew they hadn't. He knew that he had not taken a single step unwatched. He had not really believed that they would let him come this far, and he wondered why they had not killed him. Perhaps they remembered him.

There was a sound on the other side of the door.

Carey said in the antique High Martian, "Here is one who claims the guest-right." In Low Martian, the vernacular that fitted more easily on his tongue, he said, "Let me in, Derech. You owe me blood."

The door opened narrowly and Carey slid through it, into lamplight and relative warmth. Derech closed the door and barred it,

5

saying, "Damn you, Carey. I knew you were going to turn up here babbling about blood-debts. I swore I wouldn't let you in."

He was a Low Canaller, lean and small and dark and predatory. He wore a red jewel in his left earlobe and a totally incongruous but comfortable suit of Terran synthetics, insulated against heat and cold. Carey smiled.

"Sixteen years ago," he said, "you'd have perished before you'd have worn that."

"Corruption. Nothing corrupts like comfort, unless it's kindness." Derech sighed. "I knew it was a mistake to let you save my neck that time. Sooner or later you'd claim payment. Well, now that I have let you in, you might as well sit down." He poured wine into a cup of alabaster worn thin as an eggshell and handed it to Carey. They drank, somberly, in silence. The flickering lamplight showed the shadows and the deep lines in Carey's face.

Derech said, "How long since you've slept?"

"I can sleep on the way," said Carey, and Derech looked at him with amber eyes as coldly speculative as a cat's.

Carey did not press him. The room was large, richly furnished with the bare, spare, faded richness of a world that had very little left to give in the way of luxury. Some of the things were fairly new, made in the traditional manner by Martian craftsmen. They were almost indistinguishable from the things that had been old when the Reed Kings and the Bee Kings were little boys along the Nile-bank.

"What will happen," Derech asked, "if they catch you?"

"Oh," said Carey, "they'll deport me first. Then the United Worlds Court will try me, and they can't do anything but find me guilty. They'll hand me over to Earth for punishment, and there will be further investigations and penalties and fines and I'll be a thoroughly broken man when they've finished, and sorry enough for it. Though I think they'll be sorrier in the long run."

"That won't help matters any," said Derech.

"No."

"Why," asked Derech, "why is it that they will not listen?"

"Because they know that they are right."

Derech said an evil word.

"But they do. I've sabotaged the Rehabilitation Project as much as I possibly could. I've rechanneled funds and misdirected orders so they're almost two years behind schedule. These are the things they'll try me for. But my real crime is that I have questioned Goodness and the works thereof. Murder they might forgive me, but not that."

He added wearily, "You'll have to decide quickly. The UW boys are working closely with the Council of City-States, and Jekkara is no longer untouchable. It's also the first place they'll look for me."

"I wondered if that had occurred to you." Derech frowned. "That doesn't bother me. What does bother me is that I know where you want to go. We tried it once, remember? We ran for our lives across that damned desert. Four solid days and nights." He shivered.

"Send me as far as Barrakesh. I can disappear there, join a southbound caravan. I intend to go alone."

"If you intend to kill yourself, why not do it here in comfort and among friends? Let me think," Derech said. "Let me count my years and my treasure and weigh them against a probable yard of sand."

Flames hissed softly around the coals in the brazier. Outside, the wind got up and started its ancient work, rubbing the house walls with tiny grains of dust, rounding off the corners, hollowing the window-places. All over Mars the wind did this, to huts and palaces, to mountains and the small burrow-heaps of animals, laboring patiently toward a day when the whole face of the planet should be one smooth level sea of dust. Only lately new structures of metal and plastic had appeared beside some of the old stone cities. They resisted the wearing sand. They seemed prepared to stay forever. And Carey fancied that he could hear the old wind laughing as it went.

There was a scratching against the closed shutter in the back wall, followed by a rapid drumming of fingertips. Derech rose, his face suddenly alert. He rapped twice on the shutter to say that he understood and then turned to Carey. "Finish your wine."

He took the cup and went into another room with it. Carey stood up. Mingling with the sound of the wind outside, the gentle throb of motors became audible, low in the sky and very near.

Derech returned and gave Carey a shove toward an inner wall. Carey remembered the pivoted stone that was there, and the space behind it. He crawled through the opening.

"Don't sneeze or thrash about," said Derech. "The stonework is loose, and they'd hear you."

He swung the stone shut. Carey huddled as comfortably as possible in the uneven hole, worn smooth with the hiding of illegal things for countless generations. Air and a few faint gleams of light seeped through between the stone blocks, which were set without mortar as in most Martian construction. He could even see a thin vertical segment of the room.

When the sharp knock came at the door, he discovered that he could hear quite clearly.

Derech moved across his field of vision. The door opened. A man's voice demanded entrance in the name of the United Worlds and the Council of Martian City-States. "Please enter," said Derech.

Carey saw, more or less fragmentarily, four men. Three were Martians in the undistinguished cosmopolitan garb of the City-States. They were the equivalent of the FBI. The fourth was an Earthman, and Carey smiled to see the measure of his own importance. The spare, blond, good-looking man with the sunburn and the friendly blue eyes might have been an actor, a tennis player, or a junior executive on holiday. He was Howard Wales, Earth's best man in Interpol.

Wales let the Martians do the talking, and while they did it he drifted unobtrusively about, peering through doorways, listening, touching, feeling. Carey became fascinated by him, in an unpleasant sort of way. Once he came and stood directly in front of Carey's crevice in the wall. Carey was afraid to breathe, and he had a dreadful notion that Wales would suddenly turn about and look straight in at him through the crack.

The senior Martian, a middle-aged man with an able look about him, was giving Derech a briefing on the penalties that awaited him if he harbored a fugitive or withheld information. Carey thought that he was being too heavy about it. Even five years ago he would not have dared to show his face in Jekkara.

He could picture Derech listening amiably, lounging against something and playing with the jewel in his ear. Finally Derech got bored with it and said without heat, "Because of our geographical position, we have been exposed to the New Culture." The capitals were his. "We have made adjustments to it. But this is still Jekkara and you're here on sufferance, no more. Please don't forget it."

Wales spoke, deftly forestalling any comment from the City-State. "You've been Carey's friend for many years, haven't you?"

"We robbed tombs together in the old days."

" 'Archaeological research' is a nicer term, I should think."

"My very ancient and perfectly honorable guild never used it. But I'm an honest trader now, and Carey doesn't come here."

He might have added a qualifying "often," but he did not.

THE ROAD TO SINHARAT

The City-State said derisively, "He has or will come here now."

"Why?" asked Derech.

"He needs help. Where else could he go for it?"

"Anywhere. He has many friends. And he knows Mars better than most Martians, probably a damn sight better than you do."

"But," said Wales quietly, "outside of the City-states all Earthmen are being hunted down like rabbits, if they're foolish enough to stay. For Carey's sake, if you know where he is, tell us. Otherwise he is almost certain to die."

"He's a grown man," Derech said. "He must carry his own load."

"He's carrying too much..." Wales said, and then broke off. There was a sudden gabble of talk, both in the room and outside. Everybody moved toward the door, out of Carey's vision, except Derech, who moved into it, relaxed and languid and infuriatingly self-assured. Carey could not hear the sound that had drawn the others but he judged that another flier was landing. In a few minutes Wales and the others came back, and now there were some new people with them. Carey squirmed and craned, getting closer to the crack, and he saw Alan Woodthorpe, his superior, Administrator of the Rehabilitation Project for Mars, and probably the most influential man on the planet. Carey knew that he must have rushed across a thousand miles of desert from his headquarters at Kahora, just to be here at this moment.

Carey was flattered and deeply moved.

Woodthorpe introduced himself to Derech. He was disarmingly simple and friendly in his approach, a man driven and wearied by many vital matters but never forgetting to be warm, gracious, and human. And the devil of it was that he was exactly what he appeared to be. That was what made dealing with him so impossibly difficult.

Derech said, smiling a little, "Don't stray away from your guards."

"Why is it?" Woodthorpe asked. "Why this hostility? If only your people would understand that we're trying to help them."

"They understand that perfectly," Derech said. "What they can't understand is why, when they have thanked you politely and explained that they neither need nor want your help, you still refuse to leave them alone."

"Because we know what we can do for them! They're destitute now. We can make them rich, in water, in arable land, in power—we can change their whole way of life. Primitive people are notoriously resistant to change, but in time they'll realize..."

"Primitive?" said Derech.

"Oh, not the Low Canallers," said Woodthorpe quickly. "Your civilization was flourishing, I know, when Proconsul was still wondering whether or not to climb down out of his tree. For that very reason I cannot understand why you side with the Drylanders."

Derech said, "Mars is an old, cranky, dried-up world, but we understand her. We've made a bargain with her. We don't ask too much of her, and she gives us sufficient for our needs. We can depend on her. We do not want to be made dependent on other men."

"But this is a new age," said Woodthorpe. "Advanced technology makes anything possible. The old prejudices, the parochial viewpoints, are no longer..."

"You were saying something about primitives."

"I was thinking of the Dryland tribes. We had counted on Dr. Carey, because of his unique knowledge, to help them understand us. Instead, he seems bent on stirring them up to war. Our survey parties have been set upon with the most shocking violence. If Carey succeeds in reaching the Drylands there's no telling what he may do. Surely you don't want..."

THE ROAD TO SINHARAT

"Primitive," Derech said, with a ring of cruel impatience in his voice. "Parochial. The gods send me a wicked man before a well-meaning fool. Mr. Woodthorpe, the Drylanders do not need Dr. Carey to stir them up to war. Neither do we. We do not want our wells and our water courses rearranged. We do not want our population expanded. We do not want the resources that will last us for thousands of years yet, if they're not tampered with, pumped out and used up in a few centuries. We are in balance with our environment; we want to stay that way. And we will fight, Mr. Woodthorpe. You're not dealing with theories now. You're dealing with our lives. We are not going to place them in your hands."

He turned to Wales and the Martians. "Search the house. If you want to search the town, that's up to you. But I wouldn't be too long about any of it."

Looking pained and hurt, Woodthorpe stood for a moment and then went out, shaking his head. The Martians began to go through the house. Carey heard Derech's voice say, "Why don't you join them, Mr. Wales?"

Wales answered pleasantly, "I don't like wasting my time." He bade Derech good night and left, and Carey was thankful.

After a while the Martians left too. Derech bolted the door and sat down again to drink his interrupted glass of wine. He made no move to let Carey out, and Carey conquered a very strong desire to yell at him. He was getting just a touch claustrophobic now. Derech sipped his wine slowly, emptied the cup and filled it again. When it was half empty for the second time a girl came in from the back.

She wore the traditional dress of the Low Canals, which Carey was glad to see because some of the women were changing it for the cosmopolitan and featureless styles that made all women look alike, and he thought the old style was charming. Her skirt was a length of heavy orange silk caught at the waist with a broad girdle. Above that she wore nothing but a necklace and her body was slim and graceful as a bending reed. Twisted around her ankles and braided in her dark hair were strings of tiny bells, so that she chimed as she walked with a faint elfin music, very sweet and wicked.

"They're all gone now," she told Derech, and Derech rose and came quickly toward Carey's hiding place.

"Someone was watching through the chinks in the shutters," he said as he helped Carey out. "Hoping I'd betray myself when I thought they were gone." He asked the girl, "It wasn't the Earthman, was it?"

"No." She had poured herself some wine and curled up with it in the silks and warm furs that covered the guest-bench on the west wall. Carey saw that her eyes were green as emerald, slightly tilted, bright, curious and without mercy. He became suddenly very conscious of his unshaven chin and the gray that was beginning to be noticeable at his temples, and his general soiled and weary condition.

"I don't like that man Wales," Derech was saying. "He's almost as good as I am. We'll have him to reckon with yet."

"We," said Carey. "You've weighed your yard of sand?"

Derech shrugged ruefully. "You must have heard me talking myself into it. Well, I've been getting a little bored with the peaceful life." He smiled, the smile Carey remembered from the times they had gone robbing tombs together in places where murder would have been a safer occupation. "And it's always irked me that we were stopped that time. I'd like to try again. By the way, this is Arrin. She'll be going with us as far as Barrakesh."

"Oh." Carey bowed, and she smiled at him from her nest in the soft furs. Then she looked at Derech. "What is there beyond Barrakesh?"

"Kesh," said Derech. "And Shun."

"But you don't trade in the Drylands," she said impatiently. "And if you did, why should I be left behind?"

"We're going to Sinharat," Derech said. "The Ever-living."

"Sinharat?" Arrin whispered. There was a long silence, and then she turned her gaze on Carey. "If I had known that, I would have told them where you were. I would have let them take you." She shivered and bent her head.

"That would have been foolish," Derech said, fondling her. "You'd have thrown away your chance to be the lady of one of the two saviors of Mars."

"If you live," she said.

"But my dear child," said Derech, "can you, sitting there, guarantee to me that you will be alive tomorrow?"

"You will have to admit," said Carey slowly, "that her odds are somewhat better than ours."

II

The barge was long and narrow, buoyed on pontoon-like floats so that it rode high even with a full cargo. Pontoons, hull, and deck were metal. There had not been any trees for shipbuilding for a very long time. In the center of the deck was a low cabin where several people might sleep, and forward toward the blunt bow was a fire-pit where the cooking was done. The motive power was animal, four of the scaly-hided, bad-tempered, hissing beasts of Martian burden plodding along the canal bank with a tow cable.

The pace was slow. Carey had wanted to go across country direct to Barrakesh, but Derech had forbidden it.

"I can't take a caravan. All my business goes by the canal, and everyone knows it. So you and I would have to go alone, riding by night and hiding by day, and saving no time at all." He jabbed his thumb at the sky. "Wales will come when you least expect him and least want him. On the barge you'll have a place to hide, and I'll have enough men to discourage him if he should be rash enough to interfere with a trader going about his normal and lawful business."

"He wouldn't be above it," Carey said gloomily.

"But only when he's desperate. That will be later."

So the barge went gliding gently on its way southward along the thread of dark water that was the last open artery of what had once been an ocean. It ran snow-water now, melted from the polar cap. There were villages beside the canal, and areas of cultivation where long fields showed a startling green against the reddish-yellow desolation. Again there were places where the sand had moved like an army, overwhelming the fields and occupying the houses, so that only mounded heaps would show where a village had been. There were bridges, some of them sound and serving the living, others springing out of nowhere and standing like broken rainbows against

15

the sky. By day there was the stinging sunlight that hid nothing, and by night the two moons laid a shifting loveliness on the land. And if Carey had not been goaded by a terrible impatience he would have been happy.

But all this, if Woodthorpe and the Rehabilitation Project had their way, would go. The waters of the canals would be impounded behind great dams far to the north, and the sparse populations would be moved and settled on new land. Deep-pumping operations, tapping the underground sources that fed the wells, would make up the winter deficit when the cap was frozen. The desert would be transformed, for a space anyway, into a flowering garden. Who would not prefer it to this bitter marginal existence? Who could deny that this was Bad and the Rehabilitation Project Good? No one but the people and Dr. Matthew Carey. And no one would listen to them.

At Sinharat lay the only possible hope of making them listen.

*

The sky remained empty. Arrin spent most of her time on deck, sitting among the heaped-up bales. Carey knew that she watched him a great deal but he was not flattered. He thought that she hated him because he was putting Derech in danger of his life. He wished that Derech had left her behind.

On the fourth day at dawn the wind dropped to a flat calm. The sun burned hot, setting sand and rock to shimmering. The water of the canal showed a surface like polished glass, and in the east the sharp line of the horizon thickened and blurred and was lost in a yellow haze. Derech stood sniffing like a hound at the still air, and around noon he gave the order to tie up. The crew, ten of them, ceased to lounge on the bales and got to work, driving steel anchor pins for the cables, rigging a shelter for the beasts, checking the lashings of the deck cargo. Carey and Derech worked beside them, and when he looked up briefly from his labors Carey saw Arrin crouched over the fire-pit cooking furiously. The eastern sky became a wall, a wave curling toward the zenith, sooty ocher below, a blazing brass-color at its crest. It rushed across the land, roared, and broke upon them.

They helped each other to the cabin and crouched knee to knee in the tight space, the twelve men and Arrin, while the barge kicked and rolled, sank down deep and shot upward, struggling like a live thing under the blows of the wind. Dust and sand sifted through every vent-hole, tainting the air with a bitter taste. There was a sulfurous darkness, and the ear was deafened. Carey had been through sandstorms before, and he wished that he was out in the open where he was used to it, and where he did not have to worry about the barge turning turtle and drowning him idiotically on the driest world in the System. And while all this was going on, Arrin was grimly guarding her pot.

The wind stopped its wild gusting and settled to a steady gale. When it appeared that the barge was going to remain upright after all, the men ate from Arrin's pot and were glad of the food. After that most of them went down into the hold to sleep because there was more room there.

Arrin put the lid back on the pot and weighted it to keep the sand out, and then she said quietly to Derech, "Why is it that you have to go—where you're going?"

"Because Dr. Carey believes that there are records there that may convince the Rehabilitation people that our 'primitives' know what they are talking about."

Carey could not see her face clearly in the gloom, but he thought she was frowning, thinking hard.

"You believe," she said to Carey. "Do you know?"

THE ROAD TO SINHARAT

"I know that there were records, once. They're referred to in other records. Whether they still exist or not is another matter. But because of the peculiar nature of the place, and of the people who made them, I think it is possible."

He could feel her shiver. "But the Ramas were so long ago."

She barely whispered the name. It meant Immortal, and it had been a word of terror for so long that no amount of time could erase the memory. The Ramas had achieved their immortality by a system of induction that might have been liked to the pouring of old wine into new bottles, and though the principle behind the transplanting of a consciousness from one host to another was purely scientific, the reactions of the people from among whom they requisitioned their supply of hosts was one of simple emotional horror. The Ramas were regarded as vampires. Their ancient island city of Sinharat lay far and forgotten now in the remotest desolation of Shun, and the Drylanders held it holy, and forbidden. They had broken their own taboo just once, when Kynon of Shun raised his banner, claiming to have rediscovered the lost secret of the Ramas and promising the tribesmen and the Low Canallers both eternal life and all the plunder they could carry. He had given them only death and since then the taboo was more fanatically enforced than ever.

"Their city has not been looted," Carey said. "That is why I have hope."

"But," said Arrin, "they weren't human. They were only evil."

"On the contrary. They were completely human. And at one time they made a very great effort to atone."

She turned again to Derech. "The Shunni will kill you."

"That is perfectly possible."

"But you must go." She added shrewdly, "If only to see whether you can."

Derech laughed. "Yes."

"Then I'll go with you. I'd rather see what happens to you than wait and wait and wait and never know." As though that settled it, she curled up in her bunk and went to sleep.

Carey slept too, uneasily, dreaming shadowed dreams of Sinharat and waking from them in the dusty claustrophobic dark to feel hopelessly that he would never see it.

By mid-morning the storm had blown itself out, but now there was a sandbar forty feet long blocking the channel. The beasts were hitched to scoops brought up from the hold and put to dredging, and every man aboard stripped and went in with a shovel.

Carey dug in the wet sand, his taller stature and lighter skin perfectly separating him from the smaller, darker Low Canallers. He felt obvious and naked, and he kept a wary eye cocked toward the heavens. Once he got among the Drylanders, Wales would have to look very hard indeed to spot him. At Valkis, where there was some trade with the desert men, Derech would be able to get him the proper clothing and Carey would arrive at the Gateway, Barrakesh, already in the guise of a wandering tribesman. Until then he would have to be careful, both of Wales and the local canal-dwellers, who had very little to choose between Earthmen and the Drylanders who occasionally raided this far north, stripping their fields and stealing their women.

In spite of Carey's watchfulness, it was Derech who gave the alarm. About the middle of the afternoon he suddenly shouted Carey's name. Carey, laboring now in a haze of sweat and weariness, looked up and saw Derech pointing at the sky. Carey dropped his shovel and dived for the water. The barge was close by, but the flier came so fast that by the time he had reached the ladder he knew he could not possibly climb aboard without being seen.

THE ROAD TO SINHARAT

Arrin's voice said calmly from overhead, "Dive under. There's room."

Carey caught a breath and dived. The water was cold, and the sunlight slanting through it showed it thick and roiled from the storm. The shadow of the barge made a total darkness into which Carey plunged. When he thought he was clear of the broad pontoons he surfaced, hoping Arrin had told the truth. She had. There was space to breathe, and between the pontoons he could watch the flier come in low and hover on its rotors above the canal, watching. Then it landed. There were several men in it, but only Howard Wales got out.

Derech went to talk to him. The rest of the men kept on working, and Carey saw that the extra shovel had vanished into the water. Wales kept looking at the barge. Derech was playing with him, and Carey cursed. The icy chill of the water was biting him to the bone. Finally, to Wales' evident surprise, Derech invited him aboard. Carey swam carefully back and forth in the dark space under the hull, trying to keep his blood moving. After a long long time, a year or two, he saw Wales walking back to the flier. It seemed another year before the flier took off. Carey fought his way out from under the barge and into the sunlight again, but he was too stiff and numb to climb the ladder. Arrin and Derech had to pull him up.

"Anyone else," said Derech, "would be convinced. But this one—he gives his opponent credit for all the brains and deceitfulness he needs."

He poured liquor between Carey's chattering teeth and wrapped him in thick blankets and put him in a bunk. Then he said, "Could Wales have any way of guessing where we're going?"

Carey frowned. "I suppose he could, if he bothered to go through all my monographs and papers."

20

"I'm sure he's bothered."

"It's all there," Carey said dismally. "How we tried it once and failed—and what I hoped to find, though the Rehabilitation Act hadn't come along then, and it was pure archaeological interest. And I have, I know, mentioned the Ramas to Woodthorpe when I was arguing with him about the advisability of all these earth-shattering—mars-shattering—changes. Why? Did Wales say something?"

"He said, 'Barrakesh will tell the story.' "

"He did, did he?" said Carey viciously. "Give me the bottle." He took a long pull and the liquor went into him like fire into glacial ice. "I wish to heaven I'd been able to steal a flier."

Derech shook his head, "You're lucky you didn't. They'd have had you out of the sky in an hour."

"Of course you're right. It's just that I'm in a hurry." He drank again and then he smiled, a very unscholarly smile. "If the gods are good to me, someday I'll have Mr. Wales between my hands."

*

The local men came along that evening, about a hundred of them with teams and implements. They had already worked all day clearing other blocks, but they worked without question all that night and into the next day, each man choosing his own time to fall out and sleep when he could no longer stand up. The canal was their life, and their law said that the canal came first, before wife, child, brother, parent, or self, and it was a hanging matter. Carey stayed out of sight in the cabin, feeling guilty about not helping but not too guilty. It was backbreaking work. They had the channel clear by the middle of the morning, and the barge moved on southward.

Three days later a line of cliffs appeared in the east, far away at first but closing gradually until they marched beside the canal. They were high and steep, colored softly in shades of red and gold. The faces of the rock were fantastically eroded by a million years of water and ten millennia of wind. These were the rim of the sea basin, and presently Carey saw in the distance ahead a shimmering line of mist on the desert where another canal cut through it. They were approaching Valkis.

It was sunset when they reached it. The low light struck in level shafts against the cliffs. Where the angle was right, it shone through the empty doors and window holes of the five cities that sprawled downward over the ledges of red-gold rock. It seemed as though hearthfires burned there, and warm lamplight to welcome home men weary from the sea. But in the streets and squares and on the long flights of rock-cut steps only slow shadows moved with the sinking sun. The ancient quays stood stark as tombstones, marking the levels where new harbors had been built and then abandoned as the water left them, and the high towers that had flown the banners of the Sea-Kings were bare and broken.

Only the lowest city lived, and only a part of that, but it lived fiercely, defiant of the cold centuries towering over it. From the barge deck Carey watched the torches flare out like yellow stars in the twilight, and he heard voices, and the wild and lovely music of the double-banked harps. The dry wind had a smell in it of dusty spices and strange exotic things. The New Culture had not penetrated here, and Carey was glad, though he did think that Valkis could stand being cleaned up just a little without hurting it any. They had two or three vices for sale there that were quite unbelievable.

"Stay out of sight." Derech told him, "till I get back."

It was full dark when they reached their mooring, at an ancient stone dock beside a broad square with worn old buildings on three sides of it. Derech went into the town and so did the crew, but for different reasons. Arrin stayed on deck, lying on the bales with her chin on her wrists, staring at the lights and listening to the noises like a sulky child forbidden to play some dangerous but fascinating game. Derech did not allow her in the streets alone.

Out of sheer boredom, Carey went to sleep.

He did not know how long he had slept, a few minutes or a few hours, when he was wakened sharply by Arrin's wildcat scream.

III

There were men on the deck outside. Carey could hear them scrambling around and cursing the woman, and someone was saying something about an Earthman. He rolled out of his bunk. He was still wearing the Earth-made coverall that was all the clothing he had until Derech came back. He stripped it off in a wild panic and shoved it far down under the tumbled furs. Arrin did not scream again but he thought he could hear muffled sounds as though she were trying to. He shivered, naked in the chill dark.

Footsteps came light and swift across the deck. Carey reached out and lifted from its place on the cabin wall a long-handled ax that was used to cut loose the deck cargo lashings in case of emergency. And as though the ax had spoken to him, Carey knew what he was going to do.

The shapes of men appeared in the doorway, dark and huddled against the glow of the deck lights.

Carey gave a Dryland war-cry that split the night. He leaped forward, swinging the ax.

The men disappeared out of the doorway as though they had been jerked on strings. Carey emerged from the cabin onto the deck, where the torchlight showed him clearly, and he whirled the ax around his head as he had learned to do years ago when he first understood both the possibility and the immense value of being able to go Martian. Inevitably he had got himself embroiled in unscholarly, unarchaeological matters like tribal wars and raiding, and he had acquired some odd skills. Now he drove the dark, small, startled men ahead of the ax-blade. Yelling, he drove them in the torchlight while they stared at him, five astonished men with silver rings in their ears and very sharp knives in their belts.

25

THE ROAD TO SINHARAT

Carey quoted some Dryland sayings about Low Canallers that brought the blood flushing into their cheeks. Then he asked them what their business was.

One of them, who wore a kilt of vivid yellow, said, "We were told there was an Earthman hiding."

And who told you? Carey wondered. Mr. Wales, through some Martian spy? Of course, Mr. Wales—who else? He was beginning to hate Mr. Wales. But he laughed and said, "Do I look like an Earthman?"

He made the ax-blade flicker in the light. He let his hair grow long and ragged, and it was a good desert color, tawny brown. His naked body was lean and long-muscled like a desert man's, and he had kept it hard. Arrin came up to him, rubbing her bruised mouth and staring at him as surprised as the Valkisians.

The man in the yellow kilt said again, "We were told..."

Other people had begun to gather in the dockside square, both men and women, idle, curious, and cruel.

"My name is Marah," Carey said. "I left the Wells of Tamboina with a price on my head for murder." The Wells were far enough away that he need not fear a fellow-tribesman rising to dispute his story. "Does anybody here want to collect it?"

The people watched him. The torch flames blew in the dry wind, scattering the light across their upturned faces. Carey began to be afraid.

Close beside him Arrin whispered, "Will you be recognized?"

"No." He had been here three times with Dryland bands but it was hardly likely that anyone would remember one specific tribesman out of the numbers that floated through.

"Then stand steady," Arrin said.

He stood. The people watched him, whispering and smiling among themselves. Then the man in the yellow kilt said, "Earthman or Drylander, I don't like your face."

The crowd laughed, and a forward movement began. Carey could hear the sweet small chiming of the bells the women wore. He gripped the ax and told Arrin to get away from him. "If you know where Derech's gone, go after him. I'll hold them as long as I can."

He did not know whether she left him or not. He was watching the crowd, seeing the sharp blades flash. It seemed ridiculous, in this age of space flight and atomic power, to be fighting with ax and knife. But Mars had had nothing better for a long time, and the UW Peace and Disarmament people hoped to take even those away from them someday. On Earth, Carey remembered, there were still peoples who hardened their wooden spears in the fire and ate their enemies. The knives, in any case, could kill efficiently enough. He stepped back a little from the rail to give the ax free play, and he was not cold any longer, but warm with a heat that stung his nerve-ends.

Derech's voice shouted across the square.

The crowd paused. Carey could see over their heads to where Derech, with about half his crew around him, was forcing his way through. He looked and sounded furious.

"I'll kill the first man that touches him!" he yelled.

The man in the yellow kilt asked politely, "What is he to you?"

"He's money, you fool! Passage money that I won't collect till I reach Barrakesh, and not then unless he's alive and able to get it for me. And if he doesn't, I'll see to him myself." Derech sprang up onto the barge deck. "Now clear off. Or you'll have more killing to do than you'll take pleasure in."

His men were lined up with him now along the rail, and the rest of the crew were coming. Twelve tough armed men did not look like much fun. The crowd began to drift away, and the original five went reluctantly with them. Derech posted a watch and took Carey into the cabin.

"Get into these," he said, throwing down a bundle he had taken from one of the men. Carey laid aside his ax. He was shaking now with relief and his fingers stumbled over the knots. The outer wrapping was a thick desert cloak. Inside was a leather kilt, well worn and adorned with clanking bronze bosses, a wide bronze collar for the neck and a leather harness for weapons that was black with use.

"They came off a dead man," Derech said. "There are sandals underneath." He took a long desert knife from his girdle and tossed it to Carey. "And this. And now, my friend, we are in trouble."

"I thought I did rather well," Carey said, buckling kilt and harness. They felt good. Perhaps someday, if he lived, he would settle down to being the good gray Dr. Carey, archaeologist emeritus, but the day was not yet. "Someone told them there was an Earthman here."

Derech nodded. "I have friends here, men who trust me, men I trust. They warned me. That's why I routed my crew out of the brothels, and unhappy they were about it, too."

Carey laughed. "I'm grateful to them." Arrin had come in and was sitting on the edge of her bunk, watching Carey. He swung the cloak around him and hooked the bronze catch at the throat. The rough warmth of the cloth was welcome. "Wales will know now that I'm with you. This was his way of finding out for sure."

"You might have been killed," Arrin said.

Carey shrugged. "It wouldn't be a calamity. They'd rather have me dead than lose me, though of course none of them would dream of saying so. Point is, he won't be fooled by the masquerade, and he won't wait for Barrakesh. He'll be on board as soon as you're well clear of Valkis and he'll have enough force with him to make it good."

"All true," said Derech. "So. Let him have the barge." He turned to Arrin. "If you're still hell-bent to come with us, get ready. And remember, you'll be riding for a long time."

To Carey he said, "Better keep clear of the town. I'll have mounts and supplies by the time Phobos rises. Where shall we meet?"

"By the lighthouse," Carey said. Derech nodded and went out. Carey went out too and waited on the deck while Arrin changed her clothes. A few minutes later she joined him, wrapped in a long cloak. She had taken the bells from her hair and around her ankles, and she moved quietly now, light and lithe as a boy. She grinned at him. "Come, desert man. What did you say your name was?"

"Marah."

"Don't forget your ax."

They left the barge. Only one torch burned now on the deck. Some of the lights had died around the square. This was deserted, but there was still sound and movement in plenty along the streets that led into it. Carey guided Arrin to the left along the canal bank. He did not see anyone watching them, or following them. The sounds and the lights grew fainter. The buildings they passed now were empty, their doors and windows open to the wind. Deimos was in the sky, and some of the roofs showed moonlight through them, shafts of pale silver touching the drifted dust that covered the floors. Carey stopped several times to listen, but he heard nothing except the wind. He began to feel better. He hurried Arrin with long strides, and now they moved away from the canal and up a broken street that led toward the cliffs.

The street became a flight of steps cut in the rock. There were roofless stone houses on either side, clinging to the cliffs row on ragged row like the abandoned nests of sea-birds. Carey's imagination, as always, peopled them, hung them with nets and gear, livened them with lights and voices and appropriate smells. At the top of the steps he paused to let Arrin get her breath, and he looked down across the centuries at the torches of Valkis burning by the canal.

"What are you thinking?" Arrin asked.

"I'm thinking that nothing, not people nor oceans, should ever die."

"The Ramas lived forever."

"Too long, anyway. And that wasn't good, I know. But still it makes me sad to think of men building these houses and working and raising their families, looking forward to the future."

"You're an odd one." Arrin said. "When I first met you I couldn't understand what it was that made Derech love you. You were so—quiet. Tonight I could see. But now you've gone all broody and soft again. Why do you care so much about dust and old bones?"

"Curiosity. I'll never know the end of the story, but I can at least know the beginning."

They moved on again, and now they were walking across the basin of a harbor, with the great stone quays towering above them, gnawed and rounded by the wind. Ahead on a crumbling promontory the shaft of a broken tower pointed skyward. They came beneath it, where ships had used to come, and presently Carey heard the jingling and padding of animals coming toward them. Before the rise of Phobos they were mounted and on their way.

"This is your territory," said Derech. "I will merely ride."

"Then you and Arrin can handle the pack animals." Carey took the lead. They left the city behind, climbing to the top of the cliffs. The canal showed like a ribbon of steel in the moonlight far below, and then was gone. A range of mountains had come down here to the sea, forming a long curving peninsula. Only their bare bones were left, and through that skeletal mass of rock Carey took his little band by a trail he had followed once and hoped that he remembered.

They traveled all that way by night, lying in the shelter of the rocks by day, and three times a flier passed over them like a wheeling hawk, searching. Carey thought more than once that he had lost the way, though he never said so, and he was pleasantly surprised when they found the sea bottom again just where it should be on the other side of the range, with the ford he remembered across the canal. They crossed it by moonlight, stopping only to fill up their water bags. At dawn they were on a ridge above Barrakesh.

They looked down, and Derech said, "I think we can forget about our southbound caravan."

Trade was for times of peace, and now the men of Kesh and Shun were gathering for war, even as Derech had said, without need of any Dr. Carey to stir them to it.

They filled the streets. They filled the *serais*. They camped in masses by the gates and along the banks of the canal and around the swampy lake that was its terminus. The vast herds of animals broke down the dikes, trampled the irrigation ditches and devoured the fields. And across the desert more riders were coming, long files of them with pennons waving and lances glinting in the morning light. Wild and far away, Carey heard the skirling of the desert pipes.

"The minute we go down there," he said, "we are part of the army. Any man that turns his back on Barrakesh now will get a spear through it for cowardice."

His face became hard and cruel with a great rage. Presently this horde would roll northward, sweeping up more men from the Low Canal towns as it passed, joining ultimately with other hordes

31

pouring in through the easterly gates of the Drylands. The people of the City-States would fall like butchered sheep, and perhaps even the dome of Kahora would come shattering down. But sooner or later the guns would be brought up, and then the Drylanders would do the falling, all because of good men like Woodthorpe who only wanted to help.

Carey said, "I am going to Sinharat. But you know how much chance a small party has, away from the caravan track and the wells."

"I know," said Derech.

"You know how much chance we have of evading Wales, without the protection of a caravan."

"You tell me how I can go quietly home, and I'll do it."

"You can wait for your barge and go back to Valkis."

"I couldn't do that," Derech said seriously. "My men would laugh at me. I suggest we stop wasting time. Here in the desert, time is water."

"Speaking of water," Arrin said, "how about when we get there? And how about getting back?"

Derech said, "Dr. Carey has heard that there is a splendid well at Sinharat."

"He's heard," said Arrin, "but he doesn't know. Same as the records." She gave Carey a look, only half scornful.

Carey smiled briefly. "The well I have on pretty good authority. It's in the coral deep under the city, so it can be used without actually breaking the taboo. The Shunni don't go near it unless they're desperate, but I talked to a man who had."

He led them down off the ridge and away from Barrakesh. And Derech cast an uneasy glance at the sky.

"I hope Wales did set a trap for us there. And I hope he'll sit a while waiting for us to spring it."

There was a strict law against the use of fliers over tribal lands without special permission, which would be unprocurable now. But they both knew that Wales would not let that stop him.

"The time could come," Carey said grimly, "that we'd be glad to see him."

He led them a long circle northward to avoid the war parties coming into Barrakesh. Then he struck out across the deadly waste of the sea bottom, straight for Sinharat.

He lost track of time very quickly. The days blurred together into one endless hell wherein they three and the staggering animals toiled across vast slopes of rock up-tilted to the sun, or crept under reefs of rotten coral with sand around them as smooth and bright as a burning-glass. At night there was moonlight and bitter cold, but the cold did nothing to alleviate their thirst. There was only one good thing about the journey, and that was the thing that worried Carey the most. In all that cruel and empty sky, no flier ever appeared.

"The desert is a big place," Arrin said, looking at it with loathing. "Perhaps he couldn't find us. Perhaps he's given up."

"Not him," said Carey.

Derech said, "Maybe he thinks we're dead anyway, and why bother."

Maybe, Carey thought. Maybe. But sometimes as he rode or walked he would curse at Wales out loud and glare at the sky, demanding to know what he was up to. There was never any answer.

The last carefully-hoarded drop of water went. And Carey forgot about Wales and thought only of the well of Sinharat, cold and clear in the coral.

He was thinking of it as he plodded along, leading the beast that was now almost as weak as he. The vision of the well so occupied him that it was some little time before the message from his bleared and sun-struck eyes got through it and registered on his brain. Then he halted in sudden wild alarm.

He was walking, not on smooth sand, but in the trampled marks of many riders.

IV

The others came out of their stupor as he pointed, warning them to silence. The broad track curved ahead and vanished out of sight beyond a great reef of white coral. The wind had not had time to do more than blur the edges of the individual prints.

Mounting and whipping their beasts unmercifully, Carey and the others fled the track. The reef stood high above them like a wall. Along its base were cavernous holes, and they found one big enough to hold them all. Carey went on alone and on foot to the shoulder of the reef, where the riders had turned it, and the wind went with him, piping and crying in the vast honeycomb of the coral.

He crept around the shoulder and then he saw where he was.

On the other side of the reef was a dry lagoon, stretching perhaps half a mile to a coral island that stood up tall in the hard clear sunlight, its naked cliffs beautifully striated with deep rose and white and delicate pink. A noble stairway went up from the desert to a city of walls and towers so perfectly built from many-shaded marble and so softly sculptured by time that it was difficult to tell where the work of men began and ended. Carey saw it through a shimmering haze of exhaustion and wonder, and knew that he looked at Sinharat, the Ever-Living.

The trampled track of the Shunni warriors went out across the lagoon. It swept furiously around what had been a parked flier, and then passed on, leaving behind it battered wreckage and two dark sprawled shapes. It ended at the foot of the cliffs, where Carey could see a sort of orderly turmoil of men and animals. There were between twenty-five and thirty warriors, as nearly as he could guess. They were making camp.

Carey knew what that meant. There was someone in the city.

35

THE ROAD TO SINHARAT

Carey did not move for some time. He stared at the beautiful marble city shimmering on its lovely pedestal of coral. He wanted to weep, but there was not enough moisture left in him to make tears, and his despair was gradually replaced by a feeble anger. All right, you bastards, he thought. All right!

He went back to Derech and Arrin and told them what he had seen.

"Wales just came ahead of us and waited. Why bother to search a whole desert when he knew where we were going? This time he'd have us for sure. Water. We couldn't run away." Carey grinned horribly with his cracked lips and swollen tongue. "Only the Shunni found him first. War party. They must have seen the flier go over—came to check if it landed here. Caught two men in it. But the rest are in Sinharat."

"How do you know?" asked Derech.

"The Shunni won't go into the city except as a last resort. If they catch a trespasser there they just hold the well and wait. Sooner or later he comes down."

Arrin said, "How long can we wait? We've had no water for two days."

"Wait, hell," said Carey. "We can't wait. I'm going in."

Now, while they still had a shred of strength. Another day would be too late.

Derech said, "I suppose a quick spear is easier than thirst."

"We may escape both," said Carey, "if we're very careful. And very lucky."

He told them what to do.

An hour or so later Carey followed the warriors' track out across the dry lagoon. He walked, or rather staggered, leading the animals. Arrin rode on one, her cloak pulled over her head and her face covered in sign of mourning. Between two of the beasts, on an improvised litter made of blankets and pack lashings, Derech lay wrapped from head to foot in his cloak, a too-convincing imitation of a corpse. Carey heard the shouts and saw the distant riders start toward them, and he was frightened. The smallest slip, the most minor mistake, could give them away, and then he did not think that anything on Mars could save them. But thirst was more imperative than fear.

There was something more. Carey passed the two bodies in the sand beside the wrecked flier. He saw that they were both dark-haired Martians, and he looked at the towers of Sinharat with wolfish eyes. Wales was up there, still alive, still between him and what he wanted. Carey's hand tightened on the ax. He was no longer entirely sane on the subject of Howard Wales and the records of the Ramas.

When the riders were within spear range he halted and rested the ax head in the sand, as a token. He waited, saying softly, "For God's sake now, be careful."

The riders reined in, sending the sand flying. Carey said to them, "I claim the death right."

He stood swaying over his ax while they looked at him, and at the muffled woman, and at the dusty corpse. They were six, tall, hard fierce-eyed men with their long spears held ready. Finally one of them said, "How did you come here?"

"My sister's husband." said Carey, indicating Derech, "died on the march to Barrakesh. Our tribal law says he must rest in his own place. But there are no caravans now. We had to come alone, and in a great sandstorm we lost the track. We wandered for many days until we crossed your trail."

"Do you know where you are?" asked the Drylander.

THE ROAD TO SINHARAT

Carey averted his eyes from the city. "I know now. But if a man is dying it is permitted to use the well. We are dying."

"Use it, then," said the Drylander. "But keep your ill omen away from our camp. We are going to the war as soon as we finish our business here. We want no corpse-shadow on us."

"Outlanders?" Carey asked, a rhetorical question in view of the flier and the un-Dryland bodies.

"Outlanders. Who else is foolish enough to wake the ghosts in the Forbidden City?"

Carey shook his head. "Not I. I do not wish even to see it."

The riders left them, returning to the camp. Carey moved on slowly toward the cliffs. It became apparent where the well must be. A great arching cave-mouth showed in the rose-pink coral and men were coming and going there, watering their animals. Carey approached it and began the monotonous chant that etiquette required, asking that way be made for the dead, so that warriors and pregnant women and persons undergoing ritual purifications would be warned to go aside. The warriors made way. Carey passed out of the cruel sunlight into the shadow of an irregular vaulted passage, quite high and wide, with a floor that sloped upward, at first gently and then steeply, until suddenly the passage ended in an echoing cathedral room dim-lit by torches that picked out here and there the shape of a fantastic flying buttress of coral. In the center of the room, in a kind of broad basin, was the well.

Now for the first time Arrin broke her silence with a soft anguished cry. There were seven or eight warriors guarding the well, as Carey had known there would be, but they drew away and let Carey's party severely alone. Several men were in the act of watering their mounts, and as though in deference to taboo Carey circled around to get as far away from them as possible. In the gloom he made out the foot of an age-worn stairway leading upward through the coral. Here he stopped.

He helped Arrin down and made her sit, and then dragged Derech from the litter and laid him on the hard coral. The animals bolted for the well and he made no effort to hold them. He filled one of the bags for Arrin and then he flung himself alongside the beasts and drank and soaked himself in the beautiful cold clear water. After that he crouched still for a few moments, in a kind of daze, until he remembered that Derech too needed water.

He filled two more bags and took them to Arrin, kneeling beside her as though in tender concern as she sat beside her dead. His spread cloak covered what she was doing, holding the water bag to Derech's mouth so that he could drink. Carey spoke softly and quickly. Then he went back to the animals. He began to fight them away from the water so that they should not founder themselves. The activity covered what was going on in the shadows behind them. Carey led them, hissing and stamping, to where Arrin and Derech had been, still using them as a shield in case the guards were watching. He snatched up his ax and the remaining water bag and let the animals go and ran fast as he could up the stairway. It spiraled, and he was stumbling in pitch-darkness around the second curve before the guards below let out a great angry cry.

He did not know whether they would follow or not. Somebody fumbled for him in the blackness and Derech's voice muttered something urgent. He could hear Arrin panting like a spent hound. His own knees shook with weakness and he thought what a fine militant crew they were to be taking on Wales and his men and thirty angry Shunni. Torchlight flickered against the turn of the wall below and there was a confusion of voices. They fled upward, pulling each other along, and it seemed that the Shunni reached a point beyond which they did not care to go. The torchlight and the voices vanished. Carey and the others climbed a little farther and then dropped exhausted on the worn treads.

Arrin asked, "Why didn't they follow us?"

"Why should they? Our water won't last long. They can wait."

"Yes," said Arrin. And then, "How are we going to get away?"

Carey answered, "That depends on Wales."

"I don't understand."

"On whether, and how soon, somebody sends a flier out here to see what happened to him." He patted the water bags. "That's why these are so important. They give us time."

They started up the stair again, treading in the worn hollows made by other feet. The Ramas must have come this way for water for a very long time. Presently a weak daylight filtered down to them. And then a man's voice, tight with panic, cried out somewhere above them, "I hear them! They're coming...."

The voice of Howard Wales answered sharply. "Wait!" Then in English it called down, "Carey. Dr. Carey. Is that you?"

"It is," Carey shouted back.

"Thank Heaven," said Wales. "I saw you, but I wasn't sure....Come up, man, come up, and welcome. We're all in the same trap now."

V

Sinharat was a city without people, but it was not dead. It had a memory and a voice. The wind gave it breath, and it sang, from the countless tiny organ-pipes of the coral, from the hollow mouths of marble doorways and the narrow throats of streets. The slender towers were like tall flutes, and the wind was never still. Sometimes the voice of Sinharat was soft and gentle, murmuring about everlasting youth and the pleasures thereof. Again it was strong and fierce with pride, crying, *You die, but I do not!* Sometimes it was mad, laughing and hateful. But always the song was evil.

Carey could understand now why Sinharat was taboo. It was not only because of an ancient dread. It was the city itself, now, in the sharp sunlight or under the gliding moons. It was a small city. There had never been more than perhaps three thousand Ramas, and this remote little island had given them safety and room enough. But they had built close, and high. The streets ran like topless tunnels between the walls and the towers reached impossibly thin and tall into the sky. Some of them had lost their upper stories and some had fallen entirely, but in the main they were still beautiful. The colors of the marble were still lovely. Many of the buildings were perfect and sound, except that wind and time had erased the carvings on their walls so that only in certain angles of light did a shadowy face leap suddenly into being, prideful and mocking with smiling lips, or a procession pass solemnly toward some obliterated worship.

Perhaps it was only the wind and the half-seen watchers that gave Sinharat its feeling of eerie wickedness. Carey did not think so. The Ramas had built something of themselves into their city, and it was rather, he imagined, as one of the Rama women might have been had one met her, graceful and lovely but with something wrong about the eyes. Even the matter-of-fact Howard Wales was uncomfortable in the

41

city, and the three surviving City-State men who were with him went about like dogs with their tails tight to their bellies. Even Derech lost some of his cheerful arrogance, and Arrin never left his side.

The feeling was worse inside the buildings. Here were the halls and chambers where the Ramas had lived. Here were the possessions they had handled, the carvings and faded frescoes they had looked at. The ever-young, the Ever-living immortals, the stealers of others' lives, had walked these corridors and seen themselves reflected in the surfaces of polished marble, and Carey's nerves quivered with the nearness of them after all this long time.

There were traces of a day when Sinharat had had an advanced technology equal to, if not greater, than any Carey had yet seen on Mars. The inevitable reversion to the primitive had come with the exhaustion of resources. There was one rather small room where much wrecked equipment lay in crystal shards and dust, and Carey knew that this was the place where the Ramas had exchanged their old bodies for new. From some of the frescoes, done with brilliantly sadistic humor, he knew that the victims were generally killed soon, but not too soon, after the exchange was completed.

Still he could not find the place where the archives had been kept. Outside, Wales and his men, generally with Derech's help and Arrin as a lookout, were sweating to clear away rubble from the one square that was barely large enough for a flier to land in. Wales had been in contact with Kahora before the unexpected attack. They knew where he was, and when there had been too long a time without a report from him they would certainly come looking. If they had a landing place cleared by then, and the scanty water supply, severely rationed, kept them alive, and the Shunni did not become impatient, they would be all right.

"Only," Carey told them, "if that flier does come, be ready to jump quick. Because the Shunni will attack then."

He had not had any trouble with Howard Wales. He had expected it. He had come up the last of the stairway with his ax ready. Wales shook his head. "I have a heavy-duty shocker," he said. "Even so, I wouldn't care to take you on. You can put down the ax, Dr. Carey."

The Martians were armed too. Carey knew they could have taken him easily. Perhaps they were saving their charges against the Shunni, who played the game of war for keeps.

Carey said, "I will do what I came here to do."

Wales shrugged. "My assignment was to bring you in. I take it there won't be any more trouble about that now—if any of us get out of here. Incidentally, I saw what was happening at Barrakesh, and I can testify that you could not possibly have had any part in it. I'm positive that some of my superiors are thundering asses, but that's nothing new, either. So go ahead. I won't hinder you."

*

Carey had gone ahead, on a minimum of water, sleep, and the dry desert rations he had in his belt-pouch. Two and a half days were gone, and the taste of defeat was getting stronger in his mouth by the hour. Time was getting short, no one could say how short. And then almost casually he crawled over a great fallen block of marble into a long room with rows of vault doors on either side, and a hot wave of excitement burned away his weariness. The bars of beautiful rustless alloy slid easily under his hands. And he was dazed at the treasure of knowledge that he had found, tortured by the realization that he could only take a fraction of it with him and might well never see the rest of it again.

THE ROAD TO SINHARAT

The Ramas had arranged their massive archives according to a simple and orderly dating system. It did not take him long to find the records he wanted, but even that little time was almost too much.

Derech came shouting after him. Carey closed the vault he was in and scrambled back over the fallen block, clutching the precious spools. "Flier!" Derech kept saying. "Hurry!" Carey could hear the distant cries of the Shunni.

He ran with Derech and the cries came closer. The warriors had seen the flier too and now they knew that they must come into the city. Carey raced through the narrow twisting street that led to the square. When he came into it he could see the flier hanging on its rotors about thirty feet overhead, very ginger about coming down in that cramped space. Wales and the Martians were frantically waving. The Shunni came in two waves, one from the well-stair and one up the cliffs. Carey picked up his ax. The shockers began to crackle.

He hoped they would hold the Drylanders off because he did not want to have to kill anyone, and he particularly did not want to get killed, not right now. "Get to the flier!" Wales yelled at him, and he saw that it was just settling down, making a great wind and dust. The warriors in the forefront of the attack were dropping or staggering as the stunning charges hit them, sparking off their metal ornaments and the tips of their spears. The first charge was broken up, but no one wanted to stay for the second. Derech had Arrin and was lifting her bodily into the flier. Hands reached out and voices shouted unnecessary pleas for haste. Carey threw away his ax and jumped for the hatch. The Martians crowded in on top of him and then Wales, and the pilot took off so abruptly that Wales' legs were left dangling outside. Carey caught him and pulled him in. Wales laughed, in an odd wild way, and the flier rose up among the towers of Sinharat in a rattle of flung spears.

LEIGH BRACKETT

The technicians had had trouble regearing their equipment to the Rama microtapes. The results were still far from perfect, but the United Worlds Planetary Assistance Committee, hastily assembled at Kahora, were not interested in perfection. They were Alan Woodthorpe's superiors, and they had a decision to make, and little time in which to make it. The great tide was beginning to roll north out of the Drylands, moving at the steady marching pace of the desert beasts. And Woodthorpe could no longer blame this all on Carey.

Looking subdued and rather frightened, Woodthorpe sat beside Carey in the chamber where the hearing was being held. Derech was there, and Wales, and some high brass from the City-States who were getting afraid for their borders, and two Dryland chiefs who knew Carey as Carey, not as a tribesman, and trusted him enough to come in. Carey thought bitterly that this hearing should have been held long ago. Only the Committee had not understood the potential seriousness of the situation. They had been told, plainly and often. But they had preferred to believe experts like Woodthorpe rather than men like Carey, who had some specialized knowledge but were not trained to evaluate the undertaking as a whole.

Now in a more chastened mood they watched as Carey's tapes went whispering through the projectors.

They saw an island city in a blue sea. People moved in its streets. There were ships in its harbors and the sounds of life. Only the sea had shrunk down from the tops of the coral cliffs. The lagoon was a shallow lake wide-rimmed with beaches, and the outer reef stood bare above a feeble surf. A man's voice spoke in the ancient High Martian, somewhat distorted by the reproduction and blurred by the voice of a translator speaking Esperanto. Carey shut his ears to everything but the voice, the man, who spoke across the years.

THE ROAD TO SINHARAT

"Nature grins at us these days, reminding us that even planets die. We, who have loved life so much that we have taken the lives of countless others in order to retain it, can now see the beginning of our inevitable end. Even though this may yet be thousands of years in the future, the thought of it has had strange effects. For the first time some of our people are voluntarily choosing death. Others demand younger and younger hosts, and change them constantly. Most of us have come to have some feeling of remorse, not for our immortality but for the method by which we achieved it.

"One murder can be remembered and regretted. Ten thousand murders become as meaningless as ten thousand love affairs or ten thousand games of chess. Time and repetition grind them all to the same dust. Yet now we do regret, and a naive passion has come to us, a passion to be forgiven, if not by our victims then perhaps by ourselves.

"Thus our great project is undertaken. The people of Kharif, because their coasts are accessible and their young people exceptionally handsome and sturdy, have suffered more from us than any other single nation. We will try to make some restitution."

The scene shifted from Sinharat to a desolated stretch of desert coastline beside the shrunken sea. The land had once been populous. There were the remains of cities and towns, connected by paved roads. There had been factories and power stations, all the appurtenances of an advanced technology. These were now rusting away, and the wind blew ocher dust to bury them.

"For a hundred years," said the Rama voice, "it has not rained."

There was an oasis, with wells of good water. Tall brown-haired men and women worked the well-sweeps, irrigating fields of considerable extent. There was a village of neat huts, housing perhaps a thousand people.

"Mother Mars has killed far more of her children than we. The fortunate survivors live in 'cities' like these. The less fortunate..."

A long line of beasts and hooded human shapes moved across a bitter wasteland. And the Dryland chiefs cried out, "Our people!"

"We will give them water again." said the Rama voice.

The spool ended. In the brief interval before the next one began, Woodthorpe coughed uneasily and muttered, "This was all long ago, Carey. The winds of change..."

"Are blowing up a real storm, Woodthorpe. You'll see why."

The tapes began again. A huge plant now stood at the edge of the sea, distilling fresh water from the salt. A settlement had sprung up beside it, with fields and plantations of young trees.

"It has gone well," said the Rama voice. "It will go better with time, for their short generations move quickly."

The settlement became a city. The population grew, spread, built more cities, planted more crops. The land flourished.

"Many thousands live," the Rama said, "who would otherwise not have been born. We have repaid our murders."

The spool ended.

Woodthorpe said, "But we're not trying to atone for anything. We..."

"If my house burns down," said Carey, "I do not greatly care whether it was by a stroke of lightning, deliberate arson, or a child playing with matches. The end result is the same."

The third spool began.

A different voice spoke now. Carey wondered if the owner of the first had chosen death himself, or simply lacked the heart to go on with the record. The distilling plant was wearing out and metals for repair were poor and difficult to find. The solar batteries could not be replaced. The stream of water dwindled. Crops died. There was famine and panic, and then the pumps stopped altogether and the cities were stranded like the hulks of ships in dry harbors.

The Rama voice said, "These are the consequences of the one kind act we have ever done. Now these thousands that we called into life must die as their forebears did. The cruel laws of survival that we caused them to forget are all to be learned again. They had suffered once, and mastered it, and were content. Now there is nothing we can do to help. We can only stand and watch."

"Shut it off," said Woodthorpe.

"No," said Carey, "see it out."

They saw it out.

"Now," said Carey, "I will remind you that Kharif was the homeland from which most of the Drylands were settled." He was speaking to the Committee more than to Woodthorpe. "These so-called primitives have been through all this before, and they have long memories. Their tribal legends are explicit about what happened to them the last time they put their trust in the transitory works of men. Now can you understand why they're so determined to fight?"

Woodthorpe looked at the disturbed and frowning faces of the Committee. "But," he said, "it wouldn't be like that now. Our resources...."

"Are millions of miles away on other planets. How long can you guarantee to keep your pumps working? And the Ramas at least had left the natural water sources for the survivors to go back to. You want to destroy those so they would have nothing." Carey glanced at the men from the City-States. "The City-States would pay the price for that. They have the best of what there is, and with a large population about to die of famine and thirst..." He shrugged, and then went on, "There are other ways to help. Food and medicines. Education, to enable the young people to look for greener pastures in other places, if they wish to. In the meantime, there is an army on the move. You have the power to stop it. You've heard all there is to be said. Now the chiefs are waiting to hear what you will say."

The Chairman of the Committee conferred with the members. The conference was quite brief.

"Tell the chiefs," the Chairman said, "that it is not our intent to create wars. Tell them to go in peace. Tell them the Rehabilitation Project for Mars is canceled."

*

The great tide rolled slowly back into the Drylands and dispersed. Carey went through a perfunctory hearing on his activities, took his reprimand and dismissal with a light heart, shook hands with Howard Wales, and went back to Jekkara, to drink with Derech and walk beside the Low Canal that would be there now for whatever ages were left to it in the slow course of a planet's dying.

And this was good. But at the end of the canal was Barrakesh, and the southward-moving caravans, and the long road to Sinharat. Carey thought of the vaults beyond the fallen block of marble, and he knew that someday he would walk that road again.

.

www.ingramcontent.com/pod-product-compliance
Lightning Source LLC
Chambersburg PA
CBHW050908120626
46554CB00003B/1082